Reviews

'I really enjoyed the continuation of the story line. Awesome read!' Daniel

'The story was fantastic to read, I enjoyed the battle at the end.' Taylor (age 12)

'When I read this to my son he always wanted to see the illustrations which made it more visual and real for him' John

'This was a perfect new adventure with intriguing quotes to start each chapter' Amy

'I loved the second book as well' Jill (age 9)

'Loving this series so far. Highly recommend it, looking forward to the next one.' Tara

'It was fascinating to read, how Raiden and Arisha's relationship is developing. But also the new characters like the Wise One's.' Lorna

KNIGHT BLAZER

DEFENDER OF THE REALM

BOOK 2

DON TREY

© 2018 Trey Publishing

The moral rights of the author have been asserted

First published 2018

All rights reserved. This book or any portion thereof
may not be reproduced or used in any manner
whatsoever without the express written permission of
the publisher except for the use of brief quotations in
book reviews.

Published in the United Kingdom by Trey Publishing

London, United Kingdom

Test and illustrations © 2018 Trey Publishing

ISBN 978-0-9929187-1-2

Trey Publishing

A CIP catalogue record for this book is available from the
British Library

Also Written by Don Trey

Knight Blazer: Sword of Esoncia — Book 1

Knight Blazer: Goblet of Truth — Book 3

For my grandmama and my grandpapa

Chapters

Chapter 1

Ravarni the Wise One

'Belief is that deep conviction in oneself which lives in the
chamber of your heart. If you nurture it, it has the power
to bring miracles and magic right before your eyes.'

Luviya, Wise One of Safton, Second Age of Reason

*I have trained myself to see life unfold with
events that I didn't expect. I have learned to
love it. When I am flying I have no
knowledge of my destination. To me, it is a
joy simply to spread my wings and see where
the wind takes me. The magic is in the
unfurling of the wings. The miracle is the
unfolding of the path. This is life and I trust
it. Let the winds carry me and take me where
I need to be ...*

Deep in the forests on the outskirts of a

town called Safton, a white-bearded man strolled along forgotten paths. He wore a blue cloak and used a walking stick as he went, giving him an air of frailty. He hummed quietly to himself as he went. From his leather belt a chain dangled down from which hung a golden orb the size of a brick. It was a dragon's egg, infused with magical properties and utterly indestructible. The dragonlance was a fearsome weapon to those who knew how to use it.

Very few ventured out this way anymore, with the woods crawling with foul creatures sent by the Dark Lady to torment Esoncia and its surrounding lands. However, a Wise One may walk where he will and even though the darkness was spreading and creeping closer, Ravarni was not afraid. The Wise One of Safton was the defender and protector of his people and he would walk in his own woods, come what may.

Away from the noise and bustle of the city, Ravarni was able to think clearly. The air smelled sweeter and the gentle birdsong was a balm to his soul. He thought about the last attack on Safton by some rakshasas, evil winged creatures who served the Dark Lady.

She hid away, keeping her identity and the full extent of her powers a secret. The rakshasas ravaged the land for her, striking fear into all those who encountered them, or at least, almost all. They held no terror for Ravarni.

As he walked, he thought about his last encounter with these rakshasas. He had managed to glean some new information from the few survivors he had left alive. He knew they were planning a huge attack and it would be soon. He knew that, alone, he would be unable to stop it, but he believed that he might be able to lessen their numbers if only he could find the right place. He had been searching all morning and felt he was close.

As he came to a clearing he sensed eyes upon him. He pretended his boots had become unlaced and bent down to retie them. He listened, and sure enough he heard the rustle of bodies moving stealthily through the branches. When he stood up, he was certain that two rakshasas were spying on him.

I must be in the right place after all, he thought with a smile. He heard no more noises and he knew they must be scouts who had gone to report to their commander. Ravarni turned and followed in the direction he believed they'd taken. He was careful to be more silent than the creatures which had been tracking him, so that the rakshasas never even guessed they were being followed.

After quite some distance, Ravarni found himself in the very place he had been looking for. In the clearing ahead, he could see bricks being placed in the area. These rakshasas worked with purpose and Ravarni realised they were building something.

'What on Esoncia are they- ...?' He began but the words stopped as he recognised the markings on the stones. 'They are building a portal,' he said under his breath. He felt sick with shock. The ability to build portals between cities and planets had been lost many ages ago, or so he'd thought.

How have they got this knowledge? He wondered. It should be impossible but it was evident to Ravarni that the Dark Lady's command of the forces of evil had grown stronger than he had guessed.

It was clear to him now that they were building a secret portal through which they would march an army, right outside the walls of his beloved town of Safton. Not if I stop them, he thought angrily.

Something drew his attention. A huge beast was lumbering into the clearing. It was the size and shape of an elephant but with the head of a dog with three red eyes. Spiked horns covered the top of his head and saliva dripped from its massive jaws. Ravarni recognised it as an elecrant, something not seen in this world for many generations. A thick chain was around its neck, and two rakshasas were pulling it, trying to direct the lumbering beast to where they wanted it to go. Behind the elecrant was a cart laden with stones for the portal.

A creature of that size could have only travelled through the Portal of Caprasus, he thought. That's the only portal in this region which has the ability to reach the planet of Erinias and the Dark Lady's lair. But that is six days' walk away, and this beast pulled the cart with stone bricks all that way. Just how long had they been planning this and how could a beast of that size travel across the country unnoticed by anyone?

Ravarni watched as the lead rakshasa tugged on the chain, pulling the elecrant and its wagon in front of the portal where other rakshasas started to unload the stone. Ravarni watched, fascinated.

There was a commotion going on at the other side of the portal from where they were building. Ravarni focussed his attention that way and saw two rakshasas, evidently the scouts that had been tracking him, reporting to their overseer. From their shrieks, their gestures and what little knowledge Ravarni had of the guttural language of the rakshasas, he could tell that they were making their overseer aware that somebody was snooping close by. It was not a normal person but a Wise One. The overseer winced at the mention of a Wise One.

There are eight rakshasas and the elecrant, Ravarni thought. A suitable audience for me to make an introduction. He straightened up and stepped out into the clearing. All working ceased and all eyes turned to him.

'Greetings rakshasas! And just what are we doing here may I ask?' Ravarni made sure to lean heavily on his walking stick as he went, so it looked like he was a frail old man but the rakshasas knew differently. Ravarni's name and face were well known among the rakshasas since he had killed so many of them.

The elecrant started to howl with panic. It shook his head trying to use its horned spikes to break free from the harness that was tied to the cart. Four rakshasas swooped to the cart, using their talons to break the fastenings before the elecrant overturned the cart.

'I only said hello,' Ravarni said with a wry smile that only incensed the rakshasas further. The other four rakshasas stood in front of the elecrant, with their wings outstretching ready to launch a deadly attack at Ravarni.

'Rakshasas!' Shouted Ravarni; raising his arms as he spoke. He had to yell to be heard over the howling of the elecrant and the frightened gibbering of rakshasas. 'Don't waste your time. These are our lands, you have been misinformed if you believe that you can disturb the peace and prosperity of them. Go back to your lands for you will find only death here.'

The commander screamed at his rakshasas, urging them on. Some of the rakshasas crept forward, afraid of disobeying their overseer but clearly more frightened of Ravarni. The rakshasas next to the cart were close to breaking the harness. The elecrant roared and pawed at the ground, its eyes fixed on Ravarni.

'Ah, you want me to play,' Ravarni said with a smile. 'I thought you would never ask. Very well.'

Ravarni raised the dragonlance from where it had been hanging at his side. With a smile he started to swing the weapon around his head as he walked forward, the glowing orb rising higher with each swing. The rakshasas closest to him shrank away and the overseer behind them was screaming with rage and frustration.

Then the elecrant was cut loose. It howled in triumph and jumped over the four rakshasas in front of him, racing towards Ravarni. The Wise One began running towards the elecrant head on with exceptional speed.

The beast pounced up into the air ready to stab Ravarni with the sharp spikes which

covered its head. Ravarni jumped as well, swinging his dragonlance and just before the two of them collided in mid-air, the orb of the dragonlance hit the elecrant in the face. Crunch! The elecrant howled, spasming in pain as it fell to the ground. Ravarni merely turned his lunge into a somersault and, as he landed, he rolled and came up kneeling on one knee, his gaze slowly sweeping across the rakshasas. They stared at the elecrant which lay sprawled dead on the ground. There was no chance that any creature could defeat the power of Ravarni's dragonlance.

For a moment, there was stillness as the rakshasas gawped at Ravarni and he looked into their stunned faces, his gaze sweeping over all of them. Then, as fast as a striking snake, Ravarni rose and started to run towards the rakshasas. The glade was filled with the sound of leathery wings as the rakshasas all started to take flight at once. As Ravarni reached them, he jumped up swinging his chain, aiming for the last one taking flight. The chain of the dragonlance wrapped itself around the rakshasa's foot. It screamed and gibbered as Ravarni pulled the chain closer to him, drawing the rakshasa to him like he might pull back a bird of prey by its jesses.

The rakshasa squirmed wildly, its leathery wings beating furiously as it tried to escape. Ravarni kept pulling until he had wrestled it to the ground.

'Don't worry,' he said amiably. He raised his hand and from the undergrowth around them roots crept out, wrapping themselves around the rakshasa's arms and legs. The roots became tighter as they tied around the rakshasa's hands and feet, pulling the evil creature tight to the ground. 'I just want to ask you some questions,' said Ravarni in a low, calm voice. 'I'm not going to kill you. Well,' he added with a smile, 'not this time anyway.'

Chapter 2

Kiss of Innocence

'Love blossoms when true friendship allows you to be yourself'

Kerika, Guardian Angel of Seemeya, Second Age of Reason

Raiden awoke to darkness and for a moment, was confused as to where he was. He had dreamt he was home in his own world. He had been sitting on his own bed, listening to the banter of his brothers in the next room while he polished their swords.

As his eyes adjusted to his surroundings, Raiden realised he was in a forest, which seemed exceedingly strange. He nearly jumped out of his skin as he heard someone roll over nearby and sigh.

The dream was gradually fading and awareness of his situation was growing. He was in a different world, Gratious. He had arrived here through the Portal of Ravacore, he remembered now. He had been dreaming of a time when he yearned for fame and glory, a chance to prove himself. Now he had woken to find that he had just such a chance and so far, he was failing.

He tilted his head and saw his companion's form outlined by the dying embers of their campfire. Arisha. The name rose in his mind. Dragon Girl. But her dragon, Grafor, was gone. So was Freya, the pegasus, the Spirit of Esoncia, who carried Raiden's armour for him.

Something had woken him. What was it? As he lay there, his head feeling as if it was filled with wool, he listened hard to the noises around him. He tried to ignore the gentle sighing of the trees in the night breeze, he tried to hear what had pulled him from slumber.

The noise came again and realisation dawned. Raiden realised Arisha was crying. It was quiet and contained but her breathing gave her away with tiny sobs now and again.

Raiden lay there, wondering what to do. He guessed her pain came from the events of yesterday. She was grieving for Hiana, the Wise One of her home city Stridelea, whom they had found murdered by rakshasas.

His right arm was aching from the chill in the night air and he rubbed it thoughtfully. He too had felt sadness when he watched the life slipping away from Hiana's eyes, but it was her final words that haunted him. Hiana had believed him to be the land's saviour, the Knight Blazer. She believed he was destined to rid their land of evil.

He wasn't sure that he believed that. Sure, he had unlocked the armour and had brandished the sword, but he could feel the power that rested within the sword yet he couldn't reach it. Arisha didn't believe he was the Knight Blazer either, and somehow her lack of belief in him upset him even more than his own. Raiden had felt indebted to Arisha after she had saved him from a horde of rakshasas almost the moment he stepped through the Portal of Ravacore.

Very quietly and very carefully, as if he was approaching a frightened animal, Raiden eased himself over to where Arisha was lying on her back, only a few feet away. As he got closer, she turned her head towards him and he could see the streak of tears on her face. He paused, waiting for her to scowl or send him away with a biting remark but she simply stared at him, tears continuing to slip down her cheeks.

He moved closer still, so that they lay side by side. Her grey eyes were wide and beautiful in the moonlight. She smelt of grass and smoke and something indescribably intoxicating that Raiden could not identify.

He gently took her other hand, delighting in the feel of her soft skin against his. It smelt sweet, like honey. In the moonlight her beauty was breathtaking. His eyes fixed on her lips.

Raiden didn't think because he knew if he did, he would have no courage to act. He leaned forward and pressed his lips to hers. Raiden could taste sweet strawberries as their lips caressed each other. The kiss was gentle, tender yet full of feeling. It was a kiss of innocence, a perfect moment forever frozen in time.

When Arisha finally pulled away, Raiden didn't want to let go of the moment so he wrapped his arm around her and his thumb gently stroked her cheek. They lay side by side, still and silent, looking into each other's eyes. Arisha's breathing had slowed, her sobs soothed by his kiss. Raiden felt elated but he saw that Arisha's beauty that night was tinged with sadness so he simply held her.

Arisha rolled over turning her back to him, and for a sickening moment he thought she was rejecting him. But instead, she shuffled back against him, curling up within his embrace. She said nothing but her fingers intertwined with his. They lay there together in the still night. Raiden gradually felt Arisha's body relax against his and heard her breathing soften until she was asleep. Slumber did not claim him for quite some time afterwards and when he eventually fell asleep it was with his cheek pressed against her hair and the taste of their kiss still on his lips.

Chapter 3

Queen of Hearts

'In our greatest confusion, reaching out to something greater than ourselves will allow us to surrender our desires and find calmness.'

Desima, Wise One of Captershai, Third Age of Reason

Arisha slept briefly, the slightest sounds rousing her from slumber. Eventually, she opened her eyes and lay awake, staring at the brightening sky as dawn crept across it.

Confusion and pain filled Arisha, threatening to overwhelm her. She was a warrior; her wants and desires were simple. Find the Knight Blazer. Bring him safely to Esoncia. Take him to the Trial of the Goblet. Pray for his survival, but don't get attached.

When she first began her role of guide and protector, she had fiercely believed in the boys she had helped travel through the dangers of the land. But as each and every boy failed and perished, she had learned to distance herself. If she didn't believe in them, she wouldn't feel so much pain when they ultimately died. But Raiden's kiss changed everything – what did it mean?

She stood up and looked up at the moon. She went a little way from the fire so she would not disturb Raiden. She raised her arms in salutation and recited the incantation Hiana had told her many years ago. It was a prayer designed to bring your true lover to you, and to expose those who would try to play you false. She was so uncertain about her feelings for Raiden and his feelings for her that she needed to reach out to a greater power for help, the Lady of the Moon.

'Queen of hearts, star of the sea, bring my true lover, here to me.

Queen of hearts, star of the sea, bring my true lover, here to me.

Queen of hearts, star of the sea, bring my true lover, here to me.'

She lowered her arms, wondering whether her incantation had been heard. She glanced back to where Raiden still lay sleeping. She thought about returning to lie next to him, but her heart felt too heavy with grief, loss and guilt. She had broken one of the most sacred of rules — she had aimed her weapon at Raiden when he was defenceless. The beam, which incinerated creatures of evil, had passed straight through him. That in itself had shown her beyond doubt that he was pure of heart, yet her actions had been motivated by anger and she knew she would have to seek forgiveness for such actions.

She thought, we'll see Ravarni soon. He'll help me. Instead of returning to the fire, she disappeared into the forest to collect more firewood.

-oOo-

When Raiden awoke in the morning, he was lying alone. He sat up to find that Arisha had already rekindled the fire and was making breakfast. She had broken up some of their biscuits then mixed them with spring water and some berries to make a tasty gruel.

Above the fire hung some leftover strips of meat from their meal the night before, drying out so that they could be packed away in Arisha's bag.

Raiden stretched and wandered over to join her, trying to look nonchalant after waking up to find himself alone. Her smile of greeting was warm and even a little shy.

'We're not far away now. We should reach there by this afternoon,' she said.

'I must admit, I'm curious to see Esoncia,' Raiden said as he helped himself to gruel. Arisha looked down, avoiding his eyes and he wondered what she wasn't telling him.

Arisha had found some large flat leaves that could be moulded into a makeshift bowl when held. The food burned his hand, even through the thick leaf but it tasted good. When breakfast was over, they packed up their food and belongings and set off again.

About mid-morning, the forest path they had been following joined a larger path and a couple of miles further on turned into a road. As they walked along this wider track, Raiden saw that it bisected other roads and he realised they must be trade routes leading to and from the city.

As they drew closer to their destination, he saw tall towers beginning to rise above the trees, their conical rooftops covered in birds. The path began to lead upwards and they shortly crested a hill which allowed them to look down on the city before them.

'Is this Esoncia?' Raiden asked. 'It's not what I imagined.' For a start, it seemed too small to be the spectacular city which Arisha had said they were heading towards. It looked more like a large market town.

Arisha shuffled her feet and avoided his gaze. 'No. I have a confession to make. I've taken us a longer way round. There's someone I need to see first before we get to Esoncia. A day or two's delay won't harm us.'

'Oh. Okay. Who are we going to see?'

'His name is Ravarni. He's a Wise One.'

Chapter 4

Safton

'What does it mean to be wise? It means admitting that
there are some things you do not know.'
Leighan, High Sorceress of Scentia, Second Age of Chaos

'A Wise One? Like Hiana?' Raiden asked.
He saw Arisha flinch at the name and he
cursed inwardly. He had spoken without
thinking and was angry with himself for
causing her pain. The loss was still so raw
for her.

'Yes. Hiana lived with my clan. Most
settlements have a dedicated Wise One.
Some more than one. Ravarni is the Wise
One for Safton, just up ahead.'

They came to the great gates where
travellers were waiting to be waved through
by guards. Raiden glanced behind him and

saw that several roads like the one they'd been travelling, joined the larger main road on which they stood. Evidently Safton was a centre for trade. Standing on tip-toe and peering through the gates, he could see that the streets were lined with stalls.

A bulky figure stepped into his view and barked: 'Name!' Raiden took a step back automatically and looked up into the scarred and grizzled face of a guard. He opened his mouth to reply but Arisha pushed him aside.

'I am Arisha of Stridelea.' Raiden saw the guard's eyes widen and this time it was the guard who took a step back. His gruff voice became respectful.

'My apologies, Princess. It has been a long time ...'

'Yes, it has,' Arisha interrupted haughtily, 'so you will understand how eager I am to get into Safton and renew old acquaintances.'

The guard's eyes narrowed; Raiden could tell that, even though his pride was still smarting from his mistake of not recognising her, he did not take kindly to Arisha's tone and to Raiden's presence. The guard's eyes slid to Raiden. 'And he is . . .?' The guard asked suspiciously.

'My companion.' Arisha replied, impatiently adding before the guard could question her further, 'We are here to see Ravarni.'

The guard considered this. Raiden saw the indecision in his eyes as they flicked between him and Arisha. The guard drew himself up, his decision evidently coming down on the side of efficiency. 'I shall ensure he knows you've arrived.'

Arisha took a step forward, her voice low. 'You think he doesn't know already?' She shook her head then walked on. Raiden followed, trying not to meet the man's gaze but feeling the guard's eyes on his back until they had turned a corner.

'That's not a very good way to make friends,' Raiden commented amiably. Arisha glared at him and Raiden thought he was also about to receive the sharp edge of her tongue. Then her features softened.

'I suppose not. You don't need to be friendly when you're out in the wilderness, so you kind of lose the knack. I guess I could have been more polite, or calmer.'

'You were certainly very ... royal,' Raiden said. Arisha looked at him, an eyebrow raised. Then she started to laugh. Raiden grinned broadly.

Arisha led him through crowded streets, each rich with their own distinctive scent. There was the earthy smell of freshly shorn sheepskins, exotic spices which made Raiden want to sneeze, and the warm, comforting scent of sawdust. Everyone was shouting around them, trying to sell their wares. Raiden soon completely lost his sense of direction but Arisha strode confidently ahead of them, weaving among the stalls, diving down dark alleys and never hesitating.

Gradually, the crowds began to thin and fewer stalls lined the streets. There was a freshness to the air and Raiden was surprised when he saw a tree in the middle of the street. Behind it was another, then more, and suddenly they were in a scented garden. Raiden looked back. It was surreal to be able to see the edge of a bustling market while standing among apple trees with the soft trickle of a fountain nearby.

'This place is full of surprises,' he murmured.

'But hopefully not bad ones,' said a deep voice. Raiden turned and scanned the trees around him, but he could see no one apart from himself and Arisha. His hand went reflexively to his sword.

Arisha laughed and said, 'Oh, don't play tricks on him, Ravarni. Come out and introduce yourself. We travelled a long way to see you.'

A movement caught Raiden's eye. An old man was walking towards him along a path. Raiden was certain the man hadn't been there just moments before. The old man walked slightly bent, leaning on a walking stick made of ebony wood, yet his green eyes were alert and sparkling with warmth. His stride was confident, despite his slight limp. His free hand hovered over his belt where a chain dangled down, a large golden egg on the end of it. Raiden marvelled that the weight of it didn't topple the old man.

Ravarni shuffled to a stop in front of them, regarding them with twinkling eyes. 'You don't like my games, Princess? You want me to be polite? Like you were to the captain of the guard?'

Arisha flushed pink and her gaze dropped. 'Nothing gets past you, does it, Ravarni?'

'Thankfully, no,' said the old man with a chuckle. 'A Wise One would be a useless thing if knowledge escaped him.' He leaned over and embraced Arisha; Raiden saw that Arisha returned the hug fiercely, as if in great need of comfort.

'You find me with a busy night ahead of me — I fear we may have a visit from some of Raiden's new friends.'

Raiden stared at the old man. 'How do you know my name?'

Ravarni's eyes twinkled. 'As I said, a Wise One without knowledge is a pointless creature, young man. Perhaps you would like to know how I know about your attackers, about how your presence is causing a bit of a stir? Or how I know that you have a burning thirst? You can drink from the fountain over there, by the way. You should find crystal cups hanging beneath the spouts.'

Raiden opened his mouth to deny this, but his tongue felt dry and suddenly the thought of fresh water made his throat constrict. The old man was right — he was thirsty.

Raiden closed his mouth and narrowed his eyes. He saw only good humour in Ravarni's expression. 'Thank you,' he said cautiously, 'I am thirsty.' With a final glance at Arisha, Raiden moved towards the fountain, wondering if he was going to feel this confused for the whole of his stay in Safton.

Chapter 5

Faith and Believe

'Do not just listen to my words, read my feelings.

Understand my pain and this by itself will heal my spirit.'

Suprina, Energy Healer, Second Age of Chaos

Ravarni waited until Raiden was by the fountain reaching out for a cup before he addressed Arisha. 'It is always a pleasure to see you Princess, yet you invariably come with trouble on your heels. Tell me, what has happened? What is so important that you bring the Knight Blazer here to me instead of taking him straight to Esoncia? You could put him in even more danger than he already is.'

Arisha started walking away from the fountain, wanting to be certain that Raiden would not overhear them. When she could no longer hear the gurgle of the fountain, she said, 'I'm afraid.'

'Fear is a strong motivator,' Ravarni commented. He was giving her time to form the words she needed to express her fear. Giving her the space to feel her emotions freely without reserve.

'It's Raiden.'

'You're afraid of Raiden, Princess?'

'No. Not of him. For him. I'm afraid he will die, like the others, and ...' Her voice trailed away. They stood within the dappled shade of a cherry tree and although Arisha stared intently at the white blossom, she didn't really see it. Ravarni simply gave her space.

She thought of her words to Raiden earlier: A day or two's delay getting to Esoncia won't harm our cause. Speaking to Ravarni had been her main motive for coming here and yet she knew that part of her didn't want to reach the city. She didn't want Raiden to be swept up in the ceremonies and take the final challenge. Like all the others, her deepest fear was that he wouldn't pass the Trial of the Goblet. Her fear with the others had been that they would fail and she would have to start over again, continue her search for the true Knight Blazer. She felt sad at losing them as she would any journey companion. But there was something deeper to her feelings for Raiden and the thought of losing him made her stomach churn and her fists clench.

As all this flowed through her mind, as she tried to find expressions for her fear, a half-forgotten dream rose up. She had dreamt that she and Raiden had set up home by the stream near the cave where there was only peace and happiness.

She had seen the pillars of her home in the dream but unlike the excitement she felt whenever she saw them in the waking world, she had viewed them with sadness. She had known she could not return to her people. She had known that a lifetime of living within sight of the pillars but never being able to go through them was her penance for her sins and yet she didn't care. She didn't care because when she turned around, Raiden was sitting at the edge of a stream, fishing and lying back contentedly in the sun. He still wore his armour, but it was dusty from days spent in the field gathering in the harvest. They were farmers, they were lovers, they were friends. And they were happy.

'I think I love him.' She spoke in a whisper but even that sounded too loud to her. 'I love him, Ravarni, and I don't know that I can take him to the Goblet. I can't love him and then lose him if he's not the champion we longed for.'

Ravarni was silent for some moments, carefully considering his words. Then he said in a low, kind voice, 'Has it ever occurred to you, Princess, that of all the boys who have come through the Portal of Ravacore, you love him because he is special? Because he is the Knight Blazer?'

Arisha laughed but it was bitter. 'That seems too simple and perfect to be true,' she said. 'I feel the same hope with each new potential champion and I felt it with Raiden. Only it's grown into something different. I'm so confused, Ravarni.'

'Ah, confusion is a beautiful thing, Arisha,' Ravarni replied. She scowled at him. It did not feel beautiful. Ravarni put his arm around her shoulders and spoke with a depth of fondness that surprised her.

'My dear, your confusion makes me happy. I have seen my little Princess and how fearless she has been in defending the realm. I have seen her face down evil and protect the innocent. I have marvelled at her resilience, at her bravery and at her strength. And yet I have wondered – does my little princess feel nothing? Does she really only exist to fight and destroy?'

Arisha tried to pull away from him but he held her firmly. 'You make my fighting sound like a sin,' she said forlornly.

'No, my child. Like all of us, you do as you must to keep the evil from this world, but to let it rule your life, to let it be the only thing in your soul, is to let the evil win as much as it is to lay down arms against it. I have seen you show no mercy to your enemies and yet today I see your compassion, your love, for a boy you barely know. And that warms me more than a roaring fire in the depths of winter,' Ravarni said smiling, giving Arisha something to think about.

'But come now,' he said, releasing her and stepping away. 'Our Knight will be wondering where we have got to.' They

51

wandered back to the fountain to find Raiden looking around uneasily. When his gaze fell on them, Arisha saw the tension fall from his shoulders.

'Come!' Cried Ravarni, stepping between them and sweeping his arm up in a grand gesture of welcome. 'I have a feast prepared and you both look famished.'

'You have a feast ready? For what?' Raiden asked.

Ravarni winked at him. 'For you, of course. I have so few visitors that those I do have are worthy of celebration.'

'But how- ?' Raiden stopped. He gave a tired smile. 'Of course. Because you are not a useless being, you saw that we were coming and had a feast prepared.'

Ravarni laughed and hit him on the back. Raiden was surprised at the strength in the old man's arms. 'You fill me with confidence, my boy. Your insight will take you far. Now, I will not say it again – come! Let us enjoy and fill our stomachs.'

Raiden barely heard what Ravarni was saying as he led them away through the trees. Instead, he was watching Arisha. Every time she looked at him and their eyes met, she would hurriedly look away, yet there was a shy smile that never left her lips. Raiden wondered what had passed between her and the old man to bring about such a change in her.

Chapter 6

The Feast

'In any moment, even at the most perilous of times, we have the choice to stay calm, focussed and present in all that there is.'

Serisiya, Energy Healer of Safton, Second Age of Reason

The feast Ravarni had prepared was one of the greatest ones Raiden had ever seen. There was venison, whole chickens, even a swan dressed in its own feathers. There were eel pies, a salmon poached with delicate herbs, and tiny fish which he'd never tasted before which were served drizzled with a fragrant oil. Even the vegetables offered were a spectacular sight — artichokes decorated with edible gold, salads of green and red leaves, carrots swimming in golden butter.

Raiden ate his fill and then some more. Then they brought out the desserts – nuts glazed with honey, ripe and juicy strawberries dipped in chocolate, and delicate lemon syllabubs.

'What's that?' Raiden asked when a cheer went up as a servant brought out a tray covered with a velvet cloth.

'It's the centrepiece of the feast. I'm sure you can guess when you see,' Arisha replied with a teasing smile. The servant set the tray down and then whipped away the cloth to reveal the confection underneath. It was a tower made of solid sugar, so white it shone. Raiden thought back to the mountain he had first seen when he stepped through the Gates of Ravacore. Fondant creepers with colourful flowers crept up the side of the tower and at its summit was a piece of solid golden sugar which shone in the candlelight.

He had never seen the original, but he could guess what it was. 'That's the tower you told me about, in Esoncia,' he said, his voice an awed whisper. Arisha nodded.

Suddenly the voices of the crowd seemed muted. Raiden felt as if his head had been plunged under cold water and shivers ran down his spine. As beautiful as the centrepiece was, the thought of what it represented made him feel sick to his stomach. He knew nothing of Esoncia except what Arisha had told him and yet some sixth sense was warning him not to be deceived by the beauty.

'Are you alright?' Arisha asked, her brow furrowed with concern.

'Y-yes, I, I just need some air,' Raiden stammered. He stumbled to the open window and stood gulping down the air like a drowning man. Gradually, his hammering heart slowed and his head stopped spinning. The world around him looked and sounded normal, although a chip of ice remained lodged in his heart, reminding him of a cold fate he suddenly felt sure awaited him.

He gazed out across the town below him. The streets were empty, only dogs roaming them now, looking for scraps left from today's market. His gaze wandered over the homely lights immediately below him, to the town walls and beyond. The forest they'd travelled through was a darker black than the night sky above. It reminded Raiden of a living creature, waiting beyond the town

walls, ready to rise up and smother the humans within.

After his recent shock, looking at the forest made him uneasy so he turned his gaze upwards. There were no clouds in the sky and only a sliver of a moon but the stars shone brightly. He looked for the three planets that Ravarni had pointed out earlier that night. Colaos was dark purple, almost indistinguishable from the night sky. It was supposed to be the home of the ancient giants, dragons and other dangerous creatures. Slightly above that was Demetria, the smallest. It twinkled a merry green. But Raiden's eye was drawn to the largest of the three, the one glowing a sickly yellow. Erinias, Ravarni had called it. The old man had explained to Raiden that all the rakshasas they had encountered had come from that planet. The Dark Lady dwelt there, in her fortress at Darkdore.

'Are you thinking of my astronomy lesson, young man?' Asked a voice at his shoulder. Raiden jumped. He hadn't heard the Wise One approaching.

'Yes. I was thinking that if Erinias just winked out of existence, all of our problems would vanish.'

Ravarni chuckled. 'Life is rarely so simple or so easy. Who knows the origin of evil? Who is to say that the complete obliteration of Erinias would rid us of all vileness? All I know for sure is that there will always be evil and it is our role to strive for balance and we get to choose which side we want to be on.' He paused and Raiden glanced at him. The old man looked caught in the throes of a decision. 'Do you know the tale of the Dark Lady?' He asked.

Raiden frowned. The name dragged up memories from his journey. 'No. Hiana spoke that name, as did Arisha. Who is she?'

'Did you not ask Arisha on your journey here?' Ravarni asked curiously.

Raiden snorted a laugh. 'No. The one thing I've learned is you don't ask Arisha too many questions, not unless you want your explanation to come with a tongue-lashing.'

Ravarni laughed softly. 'Indeed, our little warrior Princess can be more warrior than Princess at times. But our bellies are full and the night is still. It is the perfect time for tales.

'We call her the Dark Lady, for no one knows her real name. It is rumoured that this Dark Lady was led by an unknown evil, that a higher, darker power saw her immorality and tempted her to explore the dark side of her mind. Her fortress, Darkdore, is on Erinias but it is a dark and barren place, so they are constantly trying to invade our lands and take Esoncia for themselves, but there is magical protection around Esoncia and pure evil cannot enter. That's why the town is so quiet — see? We have to enforce a curfew these days as the attacks are becoming so frequent. It is the same in many places. Stridelea as well has a curfew now with the death of their Wise One, Hiana.'

Raiden glanced down at the town below them. Although he could hear muted voices and see smoke curling from chimneys, now that he looked hard, he could not see any figures in the streets. He saw only one lone guard, walking through the empty marketplace, his spear and shield held ready. Raiden had many questions but before he could voice them, he was distracted by something in the sky. He stared hard at the vast canopy of stars but whatever had drawn his attention had gone again.

'What is it?' Ravarni asked, concern deepening his voice.

'I'm not sure,' Raiden said. 'I think it was — there! Look! Erinias just winked out of existence for a second. And again! Did you see?'

'I did,' Ravarni murmured. He was leaning forward on the balcony, staring intently at the sky. Then his eyes widened and he spoke hurriedly. 'I don't think it's your wish being granted though, Raiden. There's something in the sky. The beating of its wings is blocking out the stars. I've been expecting this,' he said grimly. Then he turned and called out over his shoulder: 'Quickly! To arms!'

There was a brief, shocked pause and then Raiden heard cries and shouts behind him, the clattering of discarded cutlery and feet running towards the doors. He heard but he did not see, for he was already racing towards the edge of the balcony, leaping over it to land on the roof below.

Chapter 7

Battle Ready

'There comes a time when we fall and despite our misfortune, we still have a choice: to pick ourselves up or stay lying.'

Srockia, Wise One of Scentia, First Age of Reason

There was a fight coming and he would be in the first lines of battle. He wanted Arisha and Ravarni to see his skills in battle. And most of all, he wanted to feel the power of the sword flowing through his blood and find a way to unlock the weapon's full potential. This time he was determined. Do or die, he thought.

His feet touched the ground just as Freya's hooves landed beside him. He reached out and touched the pegasus' saddle, and felt the grip of armour flowing up his arm and over his body. He was panting but with excitement rather than exertion. He reached down, grasped the sword's hilt and drew it from its scabbard. It gleamed white in the night air. Above him, as if in answer, a part of Erinias turned from yellow to orange, then a deep red. It pulsed and blazed as Raiden hurried to meet whatever flying horrors had been sent to kill them.

'Let them come,' he whispered, his voice deep and rough. Freya snorted beside him, pawing eagerly at the ground. He felt a rush of air batter down on him and for a second, he thought that one of the creatures was already bearing down on him but when he looked up he saw Grafor with Arisha perched on top.

'This way!' She called. 'We must get to the square – that is our best battleground. If we leave it too late, they will be in the town and we will be forced to fight them in the streets.' As she spoke, Raiden was vaulting up onto Freya's back and spurring her onwards. He felt rather than saw Grafor flying above them, a breeze from his wings wafting down to them. Raiden let Freya lead the way.

As they neared the deserted square, Freya slowed and Raiden jumped down. His heart was pounding with excitement and he could already feel the power of the sword flowing up his arm. They were still in a side street so he ran forward towards the square, hunched low to the ground. He knelt behind a pile of crates and peered into the square. Nothing moved. He glanced up at the sky but could only see rooftops above him. Raiden was kneeling in that street, present and ready but before he knew it, he heard the creatures arrive with three resounding booms that echoed through the vicinity.

Chapter 8

Bellcasious

'There will be struggle in our battle, the fight will be tough - for what would be the purpose of winning if not for overcoming the challenge of a worthy enemy?'

Metripous, Wise One of Utrides, Second Age of Chaos

The buildings around him shook with the force of these evil creatures landing and Raiden's very teeth seemed to vibrate with the power. His stomach somersaulted – exactly what kind of creature was he about to face?

He saw a tall figure step out of the shadows on the other side of the square and he caught his breath. With the wings, he had expected more rakshasas or possibly some evil variant of his own pegasus. He watched as another figure stepped forward, furling its wings back while it stretched impossibly large pectoral muscles. As a third figure walked into the square,

Raiden saw that the legs of the creatures were those of bulls, as was the head, while the body and arms were those of a man. The skin of all three was the deep red of spilled blood. In the dark, he could see the crimson gleam of their hungry eyes. One carried a spear, another a club while the third hefted the weight of a massive sword in his hand.

'I hope you're ready, Raiden,' said Ravarni behind him.

'You're very good at sneaking up on people,' Raiden said, moving aside so that the Wise One could kneel next to him and observe their enemies. Ravarni just chuckled.

'Only three bellcasii?' Ravarni said quietly. 'That's unusual.'

'Isn't three more than enough?' Raiden asked, eyeing the large, dangerous creatures warily.

'Normally the Dark Lady's foes come in great strength. A single shot from my dragon lance,' he indicated the chain he was holding

with the egg on the end, 'is enough to slay at least a couple of these bellcasii, so the Dark Lady sends droves to bombard our walls. She will often send scouts in ones and twos, but they are always outside the walls – they have never landed in the town itself before. I might have to leave one for you to play with.'

'When do we ...?' Raiden began, intending to ask when they should make a move but he was cut off by a tremendous bellow as the bellcasii started a charge across the square.

'I think you have your answer!' Ravarni yelled as he leapt over the boxes like a child and began running towards the enemy.

Ravarni ran with a speed and grace Raiden would not have guessed he had. Not to be outstripped by an old man, Raiden leaped up and ran after him. He was aware of Arisha racing in on their right to join the fight.

As Ravarni ran, he was swinging his dragonlance through the air. As the first creature reached him, swinging its club round at his head, Ravarni did a graceful forward roll, neatly avoiding the arc of the club. The creature roared its rage as its momentum carried it past Ravarni, but then it fixed its attention instead on Raiden, who was running towards it as well.

Raiden heard a cry and saw Ravarni release his dragonlance at the second bellcasious. He found himself watching the weapon as it flew through the night. Ravarni had told him the name and the purpose of the weapon, but seeing it in action mesmerised Raiden. The dragon egg was pulsing with light. It connected with its target, the second bellcasious carrying the sword. There was an explosion of light, rippling out like waves. The bellcasious stumbled in evident pain but didn't go down. Raiden braced himself as the rippling light washed over him but felt nothing except a warm breeze.

Then he had no more time to think and the first charging bellcasious with the club was on him. As he ducked and dived the creature's blows, the Sword of Esoncia sang in his hands. Light spilled from it and Raiden stared at it in amazement. Then with a cry of triumph, he directed it at the creature's head, its chest, even its legs. Yet while the bellcasious seemed slowed by this attack, it did not fall.

But then one shot of light caught the creature in the knee and it stumbled to the ground, Raiden took his chance to scramble up and back off a few paces. 'Raiden!' Arisha was calling his name. He turned to find her astride Grafor, her sceptre blazing in her hand. 'Get on Freya and stay on her! There's something different about these bellcasii!'

In a flash, Freya was by Raiden's side and he vaulted onto her. In two wing beats, the pegasus was above the rooftops and Raiden was looking down on the battle. The bellcasious he had been battling was looking up at him. He saw the creature spread its wings, ready to take chase.

Don't let it get off the ground, he thought wildly. He wasn't sure if the thought came from Freya or himself but he felt the truth of it. The bellcasious braced itself, ready to fly and Raiden directed Freya towards it, screaming his rage. His whole world narrowed, darkness surrounding him with only his foe filling up his vision. He held his breath. He concentrated and focussed all his energy on channelling the power of the sword. A piercing white light, brighter than anything he'd seen before, streamed out of the sword. It ignited the dark feathers on the bellcasious' wings.

Raiden roared his triumph and turned Freya for another shot. The bellcasious was flaming and howling in pain. Raiden, with all his presence and focus, fired the sword towards the beast. This time, the light was even brighter and a lightning bolt arced straight through the beast's chest, burning straight into the ground behind it. The bellcasious sank to the ground, the club dropping from its lifeless hands. Raiden laughed maniacally, his blood on fire with the slaughter.

He turned Freya and saw Ravarni being forced back by the bellcasious with the sword. Raiden circled above, waiting for the moment when Ravarni released his weapon and as the dragon egg crashed against the chest of the beast, Raiden released the power of the Sword of Esoncia and the bellcasious went down with a scream.

Freya landed and Raiden jumped down.

'It appears I owe you my life,' Ravarni said. He looked a little shaken.

'I thought you said one shot from your dragonlance would kill them?' Raiden asked, his breath coming in ragged gasps.

Ravarni looked grim. 'It should have,' he said.

A blast of heat washed over them and Raiden turned, shielding his eyes enough to see Grafor spewing a sea of fire that engulfed the bellcasious advancing towards them. When the fire ceased, Raiden's vision was blurred momentarily by the after-image of it, but then he saw the beast hurl its spear and saw the weapon pierce Grafor's chest. The dragon went down with a scream of pain, clawing at the weapon that was lodged in his chest.

'Impossible,' Ravarni said. He looked pale and shocked. 'That bellcasious should be dead.'

'Impossible or not,' Raiden said, 'Arisha is down and we have to help her. They hurried across the square, Raiden's eyes fixed on Arisha, her body seeming tiny compared to the huge bellcasious advancing on her. He saw her hold her sceptre aloft, light building, then exploding towards her attacker. The bellcasious slowed as the beam hit it, but did not stop. The beam ended as Arisha staggered, evidently suffering as her dragon writhed on the ground in agony. Raiden thought of his mind connection with Freya, how she had felt his pain and realised with horror that Arisha must be feeling Grafor's pain as well.

The bellcasious reached out for Arisha, its hands only inches away from her throat. She fired her sceptre. Combined with the bolt of light from the Sword of Esoncia and the egg from Ravarni's dragonlance, it hit the evil creature from all angles. The creature screamed out in pain and the force of all three weapons hurled it into the air, flipping it over like a rag doll. It landed on the ground, already dead, the thud of its body being the last sound to reverberate in the night air.

Chapter 9

Ancient Magic

'When you think you have understood everything life has to offer, remember there's always more to understand.'

Berima, Wise of Esoncia, Second Age of Reason

Arisha sank to the ground, panting with effort. The beast had nearly bested her in her weakened state. If not for Ravarni and Raiden, it would have throttled the life from her. One question ran through her head: why hadn't her sceptre worked as expected?

Ravarni came and helped her up. She waved away his look of concern. The guards were already attending to Grafor and she left him in their capable hands. She could not provide much assistance when she was feeling his pain.

'Why didn't your weapons kill them outright like the demons?' Raiden asked as they gathered round the fallen beast. Behind them, Safton town guards were running into the square, shouting orders and heading towards the two other corpses.

'That, my friend, is a very good question,' Ravarni said. He glanced over at Arisha. 'Your friend asks interesting questions, does he not?' Arisha felt the blush rising on her face. She tried to look dismissive.

'He certainly asks enough of them,' she said. Raiden looked confused and she gave him a brief, reassuring smile. Ravarni was right – his questions were always relevant but so long on her own in the wilderness had made them irritating to her at times.

'I think the answer is here for us all to see,' continued Ravarni. 'Look!' He pointed to the bellcasious before them and, looking closer, Arisha saw his meaning.

'It's wearing armour,' she said incredulously.

'I've never seen armour like that,' said Raiden. Arisha nodded in agreement.

'I definitely don't think it's something any of us have seen,' Ravarni said. He bent down to examine the corpse although Arisha noted he was careful not to touch it. He stood up, frowning. 'It's not the armour they normally wear, that's for sure. My gut feeling is that it's this armour which is infused with some sort of dark protected magic which allowed them to resist our weapons.'

'How did they get such magical armour?' Raiden asked.

'Another important question,' Ravarni said, 'and one I will need to meditate on. I have never seen such a thing in all my years. It is true that magic is woven into the very metal of our weapons but the weapons themselves are many ages old. The art of such magic is lost to us, so I have no idea how this was accomplished. I believe the Dark Lady has unlocked the secrets to such power, and if I'm right, we are in more danger than we thought.' Ravarni's frown turned suddenly into a smile and he clapped a surprised Raiden on the back.

'It's just as well you were here, my boy.'

'Me?' Raiden asked.

'Indeed! I didn't know you were so powerful,' Ravarni continued.

'I am?' Raiden looked beseechingly at Arisha but she didn't know what Ravarni was talking about.

The Wise One laughed and led them away from the corpse. 'Why, Arisha, are you telling me that you were so engrossed in fighting that you failed to notice? Our young friend here killed a bellcasious all alone. Where we failed, he succeeded. Even though evil has grown stronger with its new found magic, our faith in goodness has reaped its rewards. We have been sent a worthy champion.'

Arisha stopped dead and stared at Raiden. 'Then that means . . .' She faltered, unable to speak the words in case speaking them turned the truth false.

Ravarni smiled at them and finished her sentence. 'That means that, if only for the briefest of moments, Raiden unlocked the full potential of the sword.'

'Then that means. . .' Arisha began again.

'Yes,' said Ravarni kindly, 'it means that he could indeed be the Knight Blazer.'

Arisha laughed again, knowing that if she didn't, she'd cry with relief. 'I never thought it could be true!' She exclaimed with true delight.

Raiden looked at her askance. 'Thanks,' he said reproachfully. Arisha just laughed again and threw her arms around him, hugging him close.

'It means there's hope,' she whispered in his ear. 'There's hope after all.'

Chapter 10

Forgiveness

'Forgiveness is a power known to only a few. The courage to use that power is within even fewer.'

Chezemial, Wise one of Esoncia, Present Day

As he packed fresh provisions into the new bag Ravarni had given him, Raiden felt elated. His doubts had vanished. He had finally unlocked the true power of the Sword of Esoncia.

True, he had only done it briefly. And, no matter how hard he thought about the fight, he could not recall exactly what it was that he'd done to bring forth such power. But he had done it nonetheless, and that alone brightened his heart.

After the battle, they had returned to Ravarni's and continued the feast until

Raiden could not keep his eyes open any longer. He barely made it to his bed before he was asleep. His slumber was long and dreamless, and he awoke refreshed to hear birdsong and find fresh water to wash with. Ravarni's feast had been elaborate, but the fare put on for breakfast was exceptional. There was bread and honey, warm, sticky porridge, fried fish with mushrooms, poached eggs and bacon. Raiden had chosen some of everything, and was certain Arisha had been grinning at him behind her hand as he shovelled it in, but he hadn't cared.

Now that he'd finished packing his bag, his stomach still felt stuffed and bulging. After their long, hungry journey through the forest, it was a welcome feeling.

Raiden hoisted the bag onto his shoulder and felt its reassuring weight. He was sad to be leaving Safton and Ravarni, but he felt more prepared now for his journey than he had ever been before.

When Raiden and Arisha left Ravarni's home, the streets were packed, this time with well-wishers rather than stall-holders. Raiden's mouth fell open at the raucous cheer that went up when he and Arisha stepped into sight. Ravarni stood behind them, ushering them on, and as they went, flowers were thrown in front of them. Hands reached out to touch them for luck, and smiling faces surrounded them.

'Guess news about your success in the fight got around,' Arisha whispered to him. He glanced over at her. She'd bathed away the dust and blood from the night's fighting. The dark circles under her eyes had receded with sleep, and her skin glowed. To Raiden, on this bright sunny morning, she looked stunning.

'Guess so,' Raiden said. He felt overwhelmed by it all – the crowds, his beautiful companion, and the growing belief in his chest that he might actually be the champion they all looked for. 'I suppose you're used to this kind of thing, being a princess,' he added, feeling a need to keep the conversation going.

Arisha laughed. He loved to hear it. 'Not quite to this extent,' she said. 'I have an older sister, and she normally receives the crowds and the praise but this is all new to me.'

'What? Your clan don't appreciate a princess warrior like you? That sounds

ridiculous. I'm sure they do.' From the dark expression that crossed her face, Raiden realised that he'd said something horribly wrong. He tried to rectify it. 'I mean ...'

'It's fine,' Arisha said stiffly. She looked at him and he saw the effort she made to smile again. 'I'll tell you about it but another time.'

They were almost at the gates now and the crowds were even more packed here than at Ravarni's. The gates were wide enough to fit three carts side by side, yet Arisha and Raiden had to squeeze through the press of people to leave Safton.

Ravarni directed them down a particular path. They walked in silence, everyone's ears ringing after the tumultuous cheers of the crowds. Ravarni walked with them until they were about a mile away from the town where they found Freya and Grafor lazing in the sun. There was a red, but healing patch on his chest where the bellcasious' spear had pierced Grafor. Raiden rushed forward to greet his pegasus but Ravarni held Arisha back, speaking to her in a low voice.

'So, Princess, do you have greater faith in yourself and your companion now?'

'I do,' she said. She smiled, but it was forced.

'But you still have doubts?' Ravarni asked.

'Not about Raiden being the Knight Blazer,' Arisha said hurriedly. 'It's just ...' She bit her lip, unused to expressing her true feelings in this way. 'It's just a doubt, about whether he will love me in return.' Ravarni looked at her, and she plunged on. 'No, there is no doubt. He does not – cannot – love me.'

'Why not, Princess?'

'Because I tried to kill him when he wore no armour when he first came into our world,' Arisha blurted out. The words burned her throat as she forced them out, yet upon speaking them, she felt as if a weight had been lifted from her. She drew a deep breath to continue with her confession. 'I used the sceptre on him in the cave when he was defenceless. It is against our lore, I know it is a grave sin.' She grasped Ravarni's hands in her own. 'Can you forgive me for it, Ravarni?'

Ravarni smiled and eased his hands out of her grip, gently holding her hands in his own. 'Princess, it is not I from whom you must seek forgiveness.'

'But you are a Wise One.'

'Wise, yes. Godly, no.'

'If you cannot help me, who can?' Arisha asked wretchedly.

Ravarni gave a quiet chuckle. 'Why, that is the easiest question you have ever put to me, Arisha. You, of course. The only person whose forgiveness you need is your own.' She opened her mouth to protest but he hurried on. 'Yes, you did wrong but you have atoned for that wrong with your own conscience. You have done everything to bring Raiden here in safety and I know you will continue to do everything to protect him and take him safely to Esoncia and through the Trial of the Goblet. You have repented, you have atoned, now you must take the final step of forgiving yourself.'

Arisha was silent. She glanced over at where Raiden was fussing over Freya, brushing some twigs out of her main. She asked, 'What about Raiden? Don't I need his forgiveness?'

Ravarni followed her gaze and considered this for a moment before answering. 'It does not seem to me that he holds a grudge against you for trying to kill him.'

'But he doesn't understand our laws. He doesn't understand what it feels ...'

'Do you think that trying to kill an unarmed person is not a sin in any world that we know of?' Ravarni cut in. 'I have no doubt that you sinned by Raiden's own standards, as well as our own and yet I am equally sure that he has forgiven you. If you doubt me, why not ask him yourself?'

Arisha hung her head. She had faced down bellcasii and survived. She had been nearly overwhelmed by rakshasas and lived. Yet the thought of admitting to Raiden what she had done, and the thought of him turning away from her in disgust, made her cold with dread.

Sensing her fears, Ravarni put an arm around her and spoke soothingly. 'Faith is stronger than fear, Arisha. You must believe in yourself and in Raiden. We are in dark times and the purity that flows in all of us can easily be tainted.'

Arisha was saved from responding by Raiden calling out, 'Is everything okay? Are you ready to go?'

'Yes,' said Arisha, recovering her commanding tone. 'We can go. Esoncia awaits. Thank you, Ravarni, for everything you have done.'

'Why, I provided only food, shelter and words,' he said amiably as he escorted Arisha over to Grafor.

Arisha was surprised when Raiden spoke her own thoughts aloud, saying, 'But that was enough and more than we hoped for, Ravarni. Thank you.'

The Wise One beamed as he stepped back and the two travellers took flight on their steeds. 'Safe journey!' He called after them as they soared into the air.

Ravarni held up his right hand and blessed them for their journey ahead.

'Child of light, child of love, blessings to you from above. Sun to greet you every day, may peace and radiance bless your way.

Child of light, child of love, blessings to you from above. Sun to greet you every day, may peace and radiance bless your way.

Child of light, child of love, blessings to you from above. Sun to greet you every day, may peace and radiance bless your way.'

Ravarni watched them until they were out of sight then with a smile and with a new determination in his step, he made his way back to Safton.

Can Raiden survive the Trial of the Goblet?

Will Raiden and Arisha admit their true feelings for each other?

Who is the Dark Lady and what is the mystery surrounding her ever-increasing power?

Continue the magical story in the next book

KNIGHT

BLAZER

GOBLET OF TRUTH
BOOK 3

DON TREY

About the Author

Don Trey is a Soul Guidance Facilitator
who helps people to discover the purpose of
their life through his Soul Plan Activation
methodology. A system based on
numerology. As an Intuitive Healer and
Money Transformation Coach, he runs
workshops and seminars to help others to
develop their intuitive awareness and to be at
peace with themselves. He has previously
worked as a Software Engineer, at the
London Stock Exchange and

CompareTheMarket.com and currently lives in London, United Kingdom.

Connect with Me

Find me on Facebook:
www.facebook.com/DonTreyKnight

Follow me on Twitter:
www.twitter.com/DonTreyKnight

Thank you for reading my book. If you enjoyed it, please take a moment to leave a review. I greatly appreciate seeing these reviews.

In gratitude!
Don Trey

Knight Blazer

Activity Books

Coming Soon

CPSIA information can be obtained
at www.ICGtesting.com
Printed in the USA
LVHW080310040619
620056LV00025B/174/P